Gabriel

Gabriel

SHARING A SMILE

FOR PAPA

—N. K.

FOR MY DAD, FOR BEING SUCH A GOOD GRANDPOP.

AND TO ALL OUR LOVED ONES WHO STILL BRING US SMILES EVEN IF THEY

ARE BEHIND A MASK OR COMPUTER SCREEN AT THE MOMENT.

—A. E.

SIMON & SCHUSTER BOOKS FOR YOUNG READERS

An imprint of Simon & Schuster Children's Publishing Division

1230 Avenue of the Americas, New York, New York 10020

Text © 2021 by Simon & Schuster, Inc.

Illustration © 2021 by Ashley Evans

Book design by Lucy Ruth Cummins © 2021 by Simon & Schuster, Inc.

SIMON & SCHUSTER BOOKS FOR YOUNG READERS and related

marks are trademarks of Simon & Schuster, Inc.

For information about special discounts for bulk purchases, please contact Simon & Schuster Special Sales at

1-866-506-1949 or business@simonandschuster.com.

The Simon & Schuster Speakers Bureau can bring authors to your live event.

For more information or to book an event, contact the Simon & Schuster Speakers Bureau

at 1-866-248-3049 or visit our website at www.simonspeakers.com.

The text for this book was set in Playtime with Hot Toddies.

The illustrations for this book were rendered digitally.

Manufactured in the United States of America

0421 WOR

2 4 6 8 10 9 7 5 3

CIP data for this book is available from the Library of Congress.

ISBN 9781534497856

ISBN 9781534497863 (ebook)

WORDS BY NICKI KRAMAR · PICTURES BY ASHLEY EVANS

SHARING A SMILE

Simon & Schuster Books for Young Readers
New York   London   Toronto   Sydney   New Delhi

The world was changing.

Everyone was wearing masks.
It wasn't just nurses and doctors,
firefighters or superheroes anymore.

"We all have to wear masks to help keep everyone safe,"
Sophie's grandpa explained.

"Just like the Hara family down the street. Remember, Sophie?

They have always worn masks whenever they go outside."

"Mr. Landon is wearing a mask now, working in his garden." Sophie remembered how she usually helped Mr. Landon water his flowers.

Would she need to wear a mask to help him now?

"The mail carrier, Sammy, too," her grandpa said. Sophie watched Sammy walk by. She thought about putting on a mask to go outside to get the letters.

Sammy waved to her, like always, but Sophie couldn't see Sammy's smile.

Sophie peeked out and saw Ms. Diaz wearing a mask while she admired the butterflies.

Jacob and Abigail wore them while riding their bikes.

Sophie thought about what fun it could be to ride her bike with them.

They looked across the street to Jenny's house.

"Is Jenny wearing one too?" Sophie asked.

Sophie waved at Jenny. Jenny waved back.

"Jenny looks scared," Sophie said to Grandpa.

"Maybe she is," Grandpa said. "It can be hard to be brave when things change. That's why we need our friends to help us."

That gave Sophie an idea.

"Are you ready to put on your mask and go out, Sophie?"
Grandpa asked.
"Not yet," Sophie said. "But I have a plan."

With her grandpa's help she went to work.

Sophie sketched and Grandpa sewed.

They worked all day and stayed up late getting every detail right.

The next morning, it was time to surprise their friends with the gifts they had made.

"Now I'm ready," Sophie said. She and Grandpa put on their masks and stepped outside.

Sophie and Grandpa walked around the neighborhood sharing their gifts:

Flowers for Mr. Landon.

For Ms. Diaz,
a butterfly parade.

Bike wheels for Jacob
and Abigail.

They handed out purple
ones, pink ones, yellow,
and green. Masks that
matched everyone's
personality.

A paintbrush for Mr. Hara,
a football for Mrs. Hara,
and of course polka dots for Kiku.

And one covered in musical notes, perfect for the mail carrier, Sammy.

Finally, they got to Jenny's house.

Sophie held up the mask
they'd made for Jenny.
A lion, to help her be brave.

She knew Jenny couldn't see her smile.

But Jenny still smiled back.

The whole neighborhood smiled back.